W9-BGJ-167

THE SWEET NELLIE NOSTALGIA
GIFT BOOKS

With Thanks & Appreciation
The Pleasure of Your Company
With Love & Affection
Motherly Devotion
I Thee Wed
A Christmas Gathering
One Swell Dad

BABY DEAR

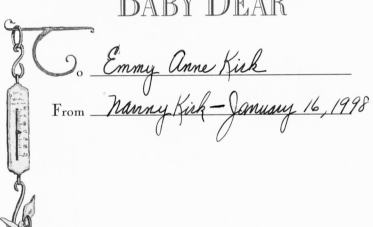

To _Emmy Anne Kirk_

From _Nanny Kirk — January 16, 1998_

*W*hen the first baby laughed for the first time, his laugh broke into a million pieces, and they all went skipping about. That was the beginning of fairies.

—*Sir James Matthew Barrie*
The Little White Bird
1902

Pat Ross

BABY DEAR

The Sweet Nellie 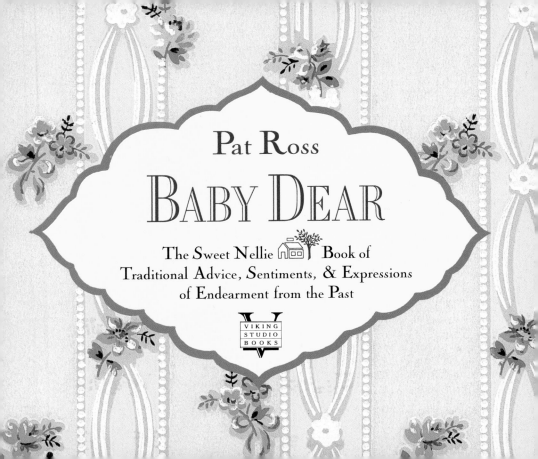 Book of
Traditional Advice, Sentiments, & Expressions
of Endearment from the Past

VIKING
STUDIO
BOOKS

VIKING STUDIO BOOKS
Viking Penguin, a division of Penguin Books USA Inc.,
375 Hudson Street, New York, New York 10014, U.S.A.
Penguin Books Ltd, 27 Wrights Lane, London W8 5TZ, England
Penguin Books Australia Ltd, Ringwood, Victoria, Australia
Penguin Books Canada Ltd, 10 Alcorn Avenue, Suite 300, Toronto, Ontario, Canada M4V 3B2
Penguin Books (N.Z.) Ltd, 182–190 Wairau Road, Auckland 10, New Zealand

Penguin Books Ltd, Registered Offices: Harmondsworth, Middlesex, England

First published in 1993 by Viking Penguin, a division of Penguin Books USA Inc.

1 3 5 7 9 10 8 6 4 2

Grateful acknowledgment is made for
permission to reprint the following copyrighted works:

"The Stork" from The Face Is Familiar by Ogden Nash. Copyright 1933
by Ogden Nash. By permission of Little, Brown and Company.
"Little" from Everything and Anything by Dorothy Aldis. Copyright 1925–1927,
© renewed 1953–1955 by Dorothy Aldis. Reprinted by permission of G. P. Putnam's Sons.
"Reflections on Babies" from Verses from 1929 On by Ogden Nash. Copyright 1940
by Ogden Nash. By permission of Little, Brown and Company.
"The Crib" from The Rocking Horse by Christopher Morley. Copyright 1919, 1947
by Christopher Morley. Reprinted by permission of HarperCollins Publishers.

0-670-84438-1   CIP data available

Printed in Mexico   Set in Nicholas Cochin
Designed by Amy Hill and Virginia Norey

AN APPRECIATION

Thoughts of a book about babies sent both family and friends in search of long-forgotten baby memorabilia stored in shoe boxes, old trunks, and the bottoms of drawers. My special thanks to all of you for the vintage birth announcements and old children's books especially.

Specific thanks go to people who are now "the regulars" when I need an extra hand, ephemera to suit the text, or good old-fashioned support: Arlene Kirkwood for her backup, and Leisa Crane for her research and constant TLC. Mary Santangelo and Berta Montgomery came through again and again with prints and wallpapers.

At Viking Studio Books, it's wonderful to have Martha Schueneman, who edits the Sweet Nellie books, executive editor Barbara Williams, and publisher Michael Fragnito. For making these books as pretty as pictures, appreciation to Amy Hill for poring through thousands of images again and again, and to Neil Stuart for the lovely jacket design.

Finally, to a very special little baby, MaryAnn Joan Marshall, who was born just as this book went to press, wishes for a happy childhood with her brother, Christopher!

AN INTRODUCTION

*B*aby, infant, bambino, bundle of joy, nursling, babe in arms, mother's angel, father's pride and joy—throughout the ages, we have filled our vocabulary with adoring names for very young children. The dictionary defines *to baby* as "to tend or treat with excessive care," with another source going even further by adding "with indulgence and often overtender care."

It seems that we all have thoughts about babyhood—our own, our child's, someone else's child's. Poets have written both eloquently and humorously about everything from parental devotion to naming the new baby. Timeless lullabies are filled with soft words, spoken or sung with gentle emotions. Nineteenth-century baby experts cautioned new parents against overdressing, overfeeding, overindulging; they advocated the teaching of proper behavior from the start. Interestingly, the commonsense attitudes of the past are frequently up-to-date even today.

My first solo outing with my new daughter was to the grocery store. The carriage, an old English pram loaned to us by a friend, was as solid as a tank and the size of a small foreign car. It wasn't rolled, it was maneuvered—into elevators whose fast doors threatened to crush us, down high curbs unkind to wheeled vehicles, through swinging door-ways designed for one, finally down the narrow aisles of our neighbor-hood grocery store. Despite the protection of the pram and her many layers of bunting, Erica looked small and vulnerable. Because grocery cartons and precarious displays kept me from wheeling the pram to the end of the aisle, I parked it mid-aisle and went the final yard or so to look for an item on the list. It was, unfortunately, sold out. As I be-gan searching frantically for some suitable replacement, I became aware of a baby crying. Preoccupied, I reached for a second-choice item when I realized that someone's baby was now working up quite a wail. Then, in the next instant, I realized that the crying baby was mine!

Our literature has always been filled with the sheer confusion and vulnerability that we feel about babies, but also the joy, the adoration, the awesome responsi-bility, the exasperation, the tenderness, the silliness, the love. We are topsy-turvy with emotion when it comes to this small someone who is totally dependent on us. *Baby Dear* passes along many of these timeless emotions through remembrances from the past.

THE
STORK CLUB

A tight little bundle of wailing and flannel,
Perplex'd with the newly-found fardel of life.

—Frederick Locker-Lampson
"The Old Cradle"
1876

*F*rom long descriptions I have heard
I guess this creature is a bird.
I've nothing else of him to say,
Except I wish he'd go away.

—Ogden Nash
"The Stork"
1936

*L*ast night the stork came stalking,
　And stork, beneath your wing
Lay lapped in dreamless slumber,
　The tiniest little thing!
From babyland, out yonder
　Beside a silver sea,
You brought a priceless treasure
　A gift to mine and me!

Last night a babe awakened,
　And babe, how strange and new
Must seem the home and people
　The stork has brought to you;
And yet methinks you like them—
　You neither stare nor weep,
But closer to my dear one
　You cuddle up and sleep.

—Eugene Field
"The Stork"
1899

*A*part from fashion and social distinction, there are a few general principles to follow in naming the baby. Take into consideration the initials! Consider the suitcase of the poor girl named Alberta Susan Spear!

—*The Mother's Encyclopedia*
1933

*N*one that I have named as yet
Are as good as Margaret.
Emily is neat and fine;
What do you think of Caroline?
How I'm puzzled and perplexed
What to choose or think of next!
I am in a little fever
Less the name I should give her
Should disgrace her or defame her;—
I will leave Papa to name her.

—Charles Lamb
"Choosing a Name"
1809

*U*ntil I was nine years old I believed that babies came from department stores.

—George Panetta
We Ride a White Monkey
1942

*T*he sponsors must make their godchild a present of some sort—a silver mug, a knife, spoon and fork, a handsomely-bound Bible, or perhaps a costly piece of lace or embroidery suitable for infants' wear. The godfather may give a cup, with name engraved, and the god-mother the christening robe and cap.

—*Our Deportment: Or The Manners, Conduct and Dress of the Most Refined Society*
Compiled by John H. Young
1879

ON THE CHILD'S CHRISTENING PARTY

It should be remembered that the baby is the person of the greatest importance on these occasions, and the guests should give it a large share of attention and praise. The parents, however, must not make this duty too onerous to their guests by keeping a tired, fretful child on exhibition.

—*Our Deportment: Or The Manners, Conduct and Dress of the Most Refined Society*
Compiled by John H. Young
1879

FAMILY
RESEMBLANCE

*Y*our mother's kin and my own vied with each other in finding family resemblances in your pudgy face. It appeared that you were a true
Van de Water. It also developed that you were a hundred percent
Gay. I wondered at their eager rivalry then. I do not understand it,
even now. You were not a pretty infant.

—Frederick F. Van de Water
Fathers Are Funny
1939

I think the tendency is to exalt maternity at the expense of paternity, to make the mother everything and the father incidental. I don't believe in that, not one bit, and I think it accounts for the large number of badly trained children.

—Ellis Meredith
Heart of My Heart
1904

*Y*ou must remember that the child of your friend is the most wonderful infant that ever came to earth to live (and if your private opinion is to the contrary it is best to keep it private), and that conventional phrases are entirely inadequate.

—Lillian Eichler
Book of Etiquette
1922

Children are poor men's riches. —French proverb

*T*he individual who has never known the joy of owning a baby has no conception of the interest which attaches to its every movement; he has no idea of the genius which is discovered in its eyes, of the precocious intellect in its method of making dirt-pies, of the music in its most frantic screams, and the beauty which parental eyes can see under a burnt skin and tow hair.

—Jennie June
Talks on Women's Topics
1864

I am the sister of him
And he is my brother.
He is too little for us
To talk to each other.

So every morning I show him
My doll and my book;
But every morning he still is
Too little to look.

—Dorothy Aldis
"Little"
1927

*H*e can't play ball with Tom and Ed
    Or skip the rope with me—
Just lies there in his little bed,
    A-cooing at us three.
But somehow, with that smile of his,
We think he's nice, just as he is.

—Madeleine Schobl
"Baby Brother"
1933

BABY'S DAY

Babies short and babies tall,
Babies big and babies small,
Blue-eyed babies, babies fair,
Brown-eyed babies with lots of hair,
Babies so tiny they can't sit up,
Babies that drink from a silver cup,
Babies that coo and babies that creep,
Babies that only can eat and sleep,
Babies that laugh and babies that talk,
Babies quite big enough to walk,
Dimpled fingers and dimpled feet,
What in the world is half so sweet
As babies that jump, laugh, cry and crawl,
Eat, sleep, talk, walk, creep, coo and all
Wee Babies?

—Attributed to Gov. F. W. Pitkin
"Wee Babies"
1882

$\mathcal{I}$t ought to be a rule in the nursery never to disturb the infant when it is happy and quiet. I have often seen a little creature, lying in its crib, cooing, laughing, crooning to itself in the sweetest baby fashion, without a care in the world to vex its composure, when in would come mama or nurse, seize it, cover it with endearments and effectually break up its tranquility. Then, the next time, when these thoughtless people wanted it to be quiet, they were surprised that it refused to be so.

—Margaret Sangster
*Good Manners for
All Occasions*
1904

*A*ll the activities of the household are now arbitrarily divided into six periods marked by bottles. There is the two o'clock bottle and the six o'clock bottle and the ten o'clock bottle. And it all starts all over again.

—J. P. McEvoy
"Six Bottles and All's Well!"
1945

*O*n a high shelf, or, better still, locked up, but handy, should be a few simple medicines for children—castor-oil, rhubarb and magnesia and a pot of jam to help these down.

—Fannie Merritt Farmer
The Boston Cooking-School Cook Book
1914

$\mathcal{M}$am-ma and Ba-by have had their break-fast, and now Pret-ty Poll shall have hers. Ba-by must not feed her, for Pret-ty Poll would take Ba-by's fin-gers for cher-ries and bite them. Mam-ma wants ba-by's fin-gers for her own kiss-es.

—Baby's Journey and Other Stories

$\int$leep. During his first year this should be
the baby's chief occupation.

—Mary L. Read
The Mothercraft Manual
1916

$\mathcal{Y}$ep, there's another one I'll recite,
And that will make twenty-eight;
Then we must surely turn out the light,
For baby, it's getting late.

—William W. Pratt
"Daddy Takes Over"
1945

$\mathcal{A}$ bit of talcum
Is always walcum.

—Ogden Nash
"Reflection on Babies"
1940

BABY'S PROPER DEPORTMENT

*A*mother once asked a clergyman when she should begin to educate her child, then three years old. "Madam," was his reply, "you have lost three years already."

—*Practical Etiquette*
1881

*T*he most important part of education
is right training in the nursery. —Plato

*Y*ou'd hardly think that the rosy chap
Sitting up there in his mother's lap,
Sweet and smiling, dimpled and fat,
Was very much of an autocrat;
Yet never a king on his throne could be
More determined to rule than he,
And a merry hubbub he's sure to make
When His Royal Highness is
    wide awake.

    —Josephine Pollard
        Apple Pie Alphabet And Other Stories
        c. 1906

*N*o well-bred child will chew his food with his mouth half open, talk with it in his mouth, or make any unnecessary noises.

—*Practical Etiquette*
1881

A simply plump, sound, rosy baby, who knows just enough to attend exclusively to its particular baby business of eating and sleeping, and does both well, is not half fast enough for this fast age.

—Jennie June
Talks on Women's Topics
1864

*R*ule 1: Start Early
  The mother, even before the little one
  is born, should visualize a well-disciplined,
  sensibly brought up infant.

Rule 2: Be Consistent
  It is a curious fact but a true one
  that young children and even babies are
  very sensitive to and appreciative of
  consistent behavior on the part of their
  parent or whoever is in charge
  of them.

—Elsie C. Mead
Good Manners for Children
1926

There was a little girl
Who had a little curl
Right in the middle of her forehead.
When she was good
She was very, very good,
But when she was bad she was horrid.

—Attributed to Henry Wadsworth Longfellow
"There Was a Little Girl"
Late 1850s

BABY
ABOUT TOWN

*H*ow proud I felt! The baby was dressed for the night without any mishaps or tears! I had only put one garment on inside-out, and had not pricked her with the diaper pins.

—Anna Roosevelt Dall
  "The Trials and Tribulations of a
  Young Inexperienced Mother
  Struggling with Her First
  Schedule"
  1932

*T*he baby cannot understand words, but it can feel the vibrations of sound, it can be impressed by the mental atmosphere, it can be influenced by the manner in which it is handled.

—Mary Wood Allen, M.D.

*O*verdressing, like overfeeding, is a common mistake.

—Mary L. Read
The Mothercraft Manual
1916

*F*ortunately for the babies of today, the frills and useless knickknacks of the last generation have gone. Every time I get out of a trunk in the attic one of my baby dresses, I wonder I was not too smothered and fussed up to live.

—Cornelia Baird Voorhis
"A Layette for $11.00?"
1932

*B*abies do not want to hear about babies; they like to be told of giants and castles, and of things which can stretch and stimulate their little minds.

—Samuel Johnson
Miscellanies
c. 1750

*C*hildren are born free and equal as far as they know. They are ready to join hands with anything that can run, or laugh, or sing, or dance, or play, white or black, straight or crooked, four-footed or biped, it is all one to them, just so the creature is alive and gifted with motion.

—*The Ideas of a Plain Country Woman*
1908

Lullabies

Father will come to his babe in the nest,
Silver sails all out of the west
   Under the silver moon:
Sleep, my little one, sleep, my pretty one, sleep.

                      —Alfred, Lord Tennyson
                        "Sweet and Low"
                        1850

If thou wilt close thy drowsy eyes,
   My mulberry one, my golden son,
The rose shall sing thee lullabies
   My pretty cosset lambkin!
And thou shalt swing in an almond-tree,
With a flood of moonbeams rocking thee,—
A silver boat in a golden sea—
   My velvet love, my nestling dove,
   My own pomegranate-blossom!

                —Eugene Field
                  "Armenian Lullaby"
                  1893

*A*nd then one night
  *W*hen the dusk was thin
I heard the nursery
  *R*ites begin:
I heard the tender
  *S*oothings said
*O*ver a crib, and
  A small sweet head.

*T*hen in a flash
  *I*t came to me
*T*hat there was my
  *I*mmortality!

—Christopher Morley
"The Crib"
1919

*T*his is the road to sleepytown—
  Barefoot highway, dusty-brown,
  Where sandman waits with blinking eyes,
Selling fresh dreams from Paradise,—
  "Who buys, who buys,
Fresh new dreams from Paradise?"

—Kenyon
Little Book of Lullabies
1898

*W*hen the Sleepy Man comes with dust in his eyes,
  (Oh, weary, my Dearie, so weary!)
    He shuts up the earth, and he opens the skies,
    (So hush-a-by, weary my Dearie.)

    He smiles through his fingers, and shuts up the sun:
  (Oh, weary, my Dearie, so weary!)
    The stars that he loves he lets out one by one
    (So hush-a-by, weary my Dearie.)

—Charles G. D. Robert
"When the Sleepy Man Comes"
1903

Sleep, little pigeon, and fold your wings,—
Little blue pigeon with velvet eyes;
Sleep to the singing of motherbird swinging—
Swinging the nest where her little one lies.

—Eugene Field
"Japanese Lullaby"
1909

Baby, flower of light!
Sleep and see
Brighter dreams than we,
Till good day shall smile away good night.

—Algernon C. Swinburne
"In a Garden"
1910

The sky is dark and the hills are white
As the storm-king speeds from the north to-night;
And this is the song the storm king sings,
As over the world his cloak he flings:
　　"Sleep, sleep, little one, sleep";
He rustles his wings and gruffly sings:
　　"Sleep, little one, sleep."

—Eugene Field
"Norse Lullaby"
1904

*I*t seems fitting that a book about traditions of the past should be decorated with period artwork. In that spirit, the art in *Baby Dear* has been taken from personal collections of original nineteenth- and early-twentieth-century cradle roll certificates, birth announcements, congratulatory cards, trade cards, advertisements, and other paper treasures of the time.

The endpapers and chapter openings contain patterns reproduced from some of our favorite vintage wallpapers.